Yesterday's Fire Engines

Superwheels & Thrill Sports

Yesterday's Fire Engines

PAUL W. HATMON

Lerner Publications Company ▪ Minneapolis, Minnesota

ACKNOWLEDGMENTS: All of the photographs in this book have been provided by Paul W. Hatmon and William A. Keith with the exception of the following: pp. 8, 16, INA Corporation; p. 21, Buffalo and Erie County Historical Society.

LIBRARY OF CONGRESS CATALOGING IN PUBLICATION DATA

Hatmon, Paul W.
    Yesterday's fire engines.

    (Superwheels and thrill sports)
    SUMMARY: Discusses firefighting equipment of the past, including hand pumpers, steamers, aerials, and service trucks and their collection and restoration.

    1. Fire-engines—United States—History—Juvenile literature. 2. Fire-engines—Collectors and collecting—Juvenile literature. [1. Fire engines—History] I. Title. II. Series: Superwheels & thrill sports.

TH9372.H37   1980   628.9'252   80-11158
ISBN 0-8225-0430-8   lib. bdg.

Manufactured in the United States of America. Published simultaneously in Canada by J. M. Dent & Sons Ltd., Don Mills, Ontario.

International Standard Book Number: 0-8225-0430-8
Library of Congress Catalog Card Number: 80-11158

1 2 3 4 5 6 7 8 9 10 90 89 88 87 86 85 84 83 82 81 80

CONTENTS

INTRODUCTION

Americans seem to have a special interest in firefighting. From the early days of the country's history, when fire engines were pulled by horses, to the age of the modern aerial truck, people have enjoyed watching firefighters do their jobs. The excitement and urgency of the fire siren have always drawn a crowd.

Fire was very common in the past because so many buildings were constructed of wood and heated by burning wood or coal. Sparks or chimney fires would start a small blaze, and the surrounding area would quickly catch fire. Even the smallest towns had some equipment on hand for fighting fires, even if it were only leather buckets kept filled with water or sand.

Today, in spite of all we have learned about preventing fires, buildings and their contents still burn. To fight these fires, modern fire departments often have whole fleets of trucks equipped with elaborate machinery. Although modern firefighting equipment is expensive and complicated, many people find it less interesting than the simpler equipment used in the past. The true fire buff is still fascinated by the fire engines of days gone by.

A fire engine from the 1920s that was restored by a fire buff

THE FIRE BUFF

"Buffs" are people with a strong interest in some subject. Their hobby is to find out all they can about their favorite subject and often to collect objects connected with it. Fire buffs are people who want to know everything there is to know about firefighting equipment. Most fire buffs have been fascinated by the sirens, flashing lights, and gleaming chrome of fire engines since they were children. They often spend their spare time at the firehouse, talking to the firefighters or looking through old photographs and fire records. Buffs also spend many hours searching for and restoring old fire equipment so that there will be a record of the history of firefighting in the United States.

Fire buffs collect many different kinds of firefighting equipment. Some are interested in small items used by firefighters in the past, for example, the brass bells that gave the alarm before modern sirens were invented. People also like to collect old brass hose nozzles or the brass lanterns that fire engines once carried. Other fire buffs specialize in accessories such as the leather helmets that firefighters used to wear or the seats from old fire engines. (One collector uses these seats in his office instead of the usual furniture.)

Another small item popular with collectors is the "fire mark." Fire marks were first used in the 1760s, when the earliest insurance companies were formed. The companies gave their members wooden or metal signs to put on their front doors or mailboxes to indicate that their homes were insured. Insurance companies often paid rewards to volunteer firefighters who fought to save one of their insured houses. Therefore, firefighters tended to concentrate their attention on houses bearing fire marks. Fire marks were used in the United States until the 1850s, when the first professional fire departments were formed and equal service went to everyone.

Fire marks *(left)* **and leather fire buckets** *(above)* **are some of the small objects prized by collectors.**

COLLECTING AND RESTORING FIRE ENGINES

Although many fire buffs collect small items such as fire marks and brass nozzles, the most serious buffs want to find and preserve an entire fire engine. These collectors have formed a club, which has members all over the United States. The list of members is growing and will soon be as long as the club name, which is the Society for the Preservation and Appreciation of Antique Motor Fire Apparatus in America. Collectors usually call the organization SPAAMFAA.

How do members of SPAAMFAA and other collectors go about acquiring fire engines? Many times, they buy them directly from fire departments. After 20 or 30 years of hard use, fire engines become worn or outdated and are often sold to the public. Sometimes, fire engines are sold because they do not meet federal or state regulations for safety. Fire buffs usually want such engines more than the junk dealers want them and will pay more. These purchases usually take place in small towns or rural areas where older, less expensive fire trucks have remained in use rather than being replaced by the complex equipment used in larger fire departments.

Because such fire engines are often used down to the very day they are sold, they are in fairly good condition and take little time or money to restore. Sometimes, however, before the engines are put on the market, they are stripped of equipment such as bells, nozzles, ladders, and axes, which could still be useful to the fire department. The buff often spends a great deal of time and effort replacing these items so that the fire engine will be complete and authentic.

Not all fire engines are in such good shape

when the fire buffs get them. Some of them may be quite worn out by the time they are released from duty. Others are abandoned in lots and simply forgotten until they are badly rusted and damaged. These abandoned fire engines, as well as some that have been specially built, are hard to restore because the equipment is no longer manufactured. For example, some of the older fire trucks used huge, hard rubber tires that are not made anymore. It is difficult to get needed parts from another truck of the same model because so many people are beginning to collect fire equipment.

The amount of work needed to restore a really old engine to its original condition can be enormous. The metal of the truck body may have been eaten away by the acid in the chemical tanks and may require much sanding and painting. A fire buff often works for hours repainting the gold stripes, designs, and scrolls as they were when the engine was new. Chrome plating must often be replaced, along with burned or unsafe wooden ladders.

Even after the restoration is complete, collectors have other problems. Old fire trucks seldom had mufflers, but they have to be added if the vehicles are going to be driven. Driving an old fire engine can be very expensive; some units get only three or four miles per gallon of gasoline. An even bigger problem is finding a place to keep a restored fire engine. Where do you park a truck 30 feet long or one with a 75-foot ladder?

In spite of the problems and the expense, fire buffs enjoy their hobby and are proud of it. They feel that it is worth all the money and effort when they succeed in restoring a machine to its original handsome appearance. After their work is finished, fire buffs are

A lot of hard work will be needed to restore this 1921 fire engine to its original condition.

ready to have fun. Members of SPAAMFAA frequently hold "musters," which is the name for gatherings called to inspect or examine something. At a muster, the club members admire and compare each other's work. They often put on shows to demonstrate how well their engines still run or how far they can send a stream of water. These shows are much like the competitions held by volunteer firefighters of the past.

A muster gives fire buffs the chance to show off their equipment and to see what other collectors have accomplished. Whether they have chosen to restore an ancient hand-pumped engine, a steam engine, or an aerial model, buffs are as proud of their machines as if each were the last of its kind left on earth. They know that their restored fire engines are an important part of the history of firefighting in the United States.

An aerial fire truck with its long ladder raised

A pumping competition at a SPAAMFAA muster

HAND PUMPERS

The earliest kind of American firefighting equipment is quite rare. What has survived is usually not found in private collections but in museums, where everyone can enjoy seeing it. Among these early firefighting tools are the large leather buckets used by the colonists in the early 1600s. When a fire was discovered, the townspeople would bring their buckets and form two lines between the fire and the nearest source of water. Buckets full of water would be passed up one line, the water thrown on the fire, and the buckets passed back down the other line to be refilled.

The use of hand-pumped fire engines brought some improvement in the American method of firefighting. In 1679 the city of Boston imported the first engine of this kind from England. A bucket brigade was still needed to fill the container on the engine that held the water. When a handle was pushed down, the water squirted out of the chamber through a nozzle.

It took many months to import the hand pumpers from England, so eventually American colonists started to make their own fire engines. They put the engines on wheels so they could be pulled instead of carried to a fire, and they attached a bell to warn people that the engine was coming. The colonists also added hoses so the firefighters could stand farther away from the fire. The greatest improvement was probably the suction pipe that allowed the water chamber to be filled directly from a well or stream rather than by means of buckets. Later, the development of water mains and hydrant systems would make it possible to draw water from an even more convenient source.

Hand-pumped engines took whole crews of workers to operate for any length of time.

Large hand pumpers were operated by teams of workers, some standing on the ground and others on platforms.

One type of fire engine had a lever with a handle on each end that was pumped by two people in a kind of teeter-totter action. It was hard work pushing against the force of the water, and the pumpers had to be replaced often. Another kind of hand-pumped engine had room for several people on each end of the lever. Some types of engines had platforms on which workers stood so that they could use their whole weight to pump the engine.

During the colonial period, there were improvements not only in firefighting equipment, but also in the system of fighting fire. By 1740 Boston and Philadelphia had organized companies of volunteer firefighters, and after the American Revolution, the idea spread to many other cities. It was hard work to pull a fire engine and to keep it pumping, but there was never a shortage of eager volunteers because of the glory associated with the job. Communities had great respect for their volunteer fire companies, and the firefighters were proud of how hard and how long they could pump. Volunteers practiced together so their company would be the fastest and most able in town.

Members of volunteer fire companies often developed great affection for their hand-pumped fire engines, despite the fact that they were clumsy and tiring to operate. The hand pumpers took on personalities of their own, and the firefighters frequently gave them names such as Mankiller or Lightning.

This elegant hand pumper from the early 1800s is decorated with a picture of Benjamin Franklin. It belonged to the Philadelphia fire company established by Franklin in the colonial period.

Volunteers became so proud of their company's pumper that they would have it decorated with silver plating, gold leaf, brass plates, or scenic paintings—all at their own expense. Putting such fancywork on an engine was a form of competition between individual volunteer companies. Each company wanted its fire engine to be more impressive than the engines of other companies.

After a time, this competition between volunteer fire companies became more than just friendly rivalry. Volunteers began to invade the territories of other companies in their eagerness to fight fires. Accidents occurred as volunteers pulling their engines tried to pass each other on the way to a fire. Companies sometimes sent people ahead to hide the fire hydrant under a barrel to keep it from being used until they arrived on the scene. On other occasions, a rival company's hose would be cut in order to gain use of the hydrant.

Volunteer companies were seldom willing to cooperate in putting out a fire. Instead of working together, they often fought with each other while the fire burned.

By the middle of the 1800s, problems with rowdy and destructive volunteers were at their worst. But developments were taking place in firefighting equipment that would soon put an end to this kind of volunteer company. In 1853 the city of Cincinnati acquired a steam-powered fire engine and created a professional, paid fire department to use it. The steam engine was not only more efficient than the hand-pumped engine, but also more complicated and expensive. It had to be operated by skilled, professional firefighters, not untrained volunteers. The use of the steam-powered fire engine soon spread from Cincinnati to other American cities, and with it came a new era in American firefighting.

The development of the steam-powered fire engine brought a new era in American firefighting.

STEAMERS

A steam engine was more efficient than a hand pumper because it used steam power rather than human power to pump water. Steam was produced by burning coal to heat water in the engine's boiler. The pressure of the steam moved pistons that pumped water from the fire hydrant. As long as there was enough coal to keep the boiler going, a steamer could pump indefinitely.

Despite their advantages, however, the new steam-powered fire engines were not welcomed by everyone. The volunteers who worked the hand pumpers hated to lose the prestige their jobs gave them, and they resisted the steamers and the professional firefighters who operated them. When the employees of the new Cincinnati Fire Department reported to their first fire in 1853, the volunteers were there to fight them for the privilege of putting out the fire. Volunteers also staged contests between their beloved hand pumpers and the newfangled machines. In 1855 one of New York's fire crews put its best hand-pumped engine up against a steam engine. The men were able to hand-pump a stream of water 5 or 10 feet farther than the steamer could, but after they were exhausted, the steamer was still pumping.

Eventually, it became clear that human muscle could not compete with steam power and that professional firefighters were more dependable than volunteers. Everyone realized that a new and better way of fighting fires had been found.

Even after most firefighters had accepted the steamer, however, there was still some resistance. The early steamers were made of cast iron and were very heavy, weighing almost 10 tons. Later models using steel and brass were lighter, but firefighters claimed that they couldn't be pulled over soft ground or bumpy roads and that wharves and wooden sidewalks would collapse under their weight. Weight was also a problem because American cities were getting bigger and more spread out. Firefighters used too much energy and time pulling the heavy steam engines to fires.

The obvious solution to the problem was using horses to pull the steamers, but firefighters were reluctant to accept this kind of help. Fire departments did not want the expense of buying and maintaining horses, and the proud firefighters did not like the idea of sharing fire stations with them. At first, fire departments rented horses from livery stables or used any that were available at the time of a fire. Eventually, however, large American communities realized that it would be to their advantage to have their own teams of well-trained horses ready at the fire stations. The romantic era of bright steam engines pulled by spirited and loyal horses had begun.

The horses used by fire departments were carefully chosen for their important job. It often took three horses to pull the heavy steamers, and the teams were matched in size so that they would pull evenly. They were also matched in color so that they would make an attractive appearance. The personality of the horse was another important consideration. There was no place in the service for an easily frightened "Nervous Nelly."

During the late 1800s, this horse-drawn steamer raced to fires in Buffalo, New York.

Fire horses were carefully trained, and they became as dedicated to their jobs as human firefighters. Injured or sick horses left in the fire house sometimes broke free and followed steam engines to a fire. When they became too old to race to fires, horses were retired and often sold as wagon horses. It sometimes happened that a delivery man would return from an errand to find his retired fire horse and his wagon clattering away after a steamer on its way to a fire.

Horses were not the only animals found around American fire stations during the last half of the 1800s. Many fire departments kept dogs as mascots to relieve the boredom of quiet times between fires. Pictures of fire houses from this period often show a dog asleep under a firefighter's chair or perched

Dogs are still found around modern fire stations. Corky, a Dalmatian, is the mascot of the Kansas City Fire Department.

on the front seat of a fire truck. Today some fire companies continue the tradition of having dogs as mascots. Dalmatians have always had a reputation as fire dogs, but almost any dog likes a fast ride on a fire engine with the wind blowing in its face.

By the end of the 1800s, the steam fire engine, pulled by prancing horses and accompanied by a barking dog, could be seen on the streets of most American cities. The average steamer of this period could pump about 500 gallons of water per minute (GPM), but some could produce 1,000 GPM, using four horses. The pumps operated with two pistons, the pressure from the steam moving first one piston and then the other. A large dome on the front of the engine, called an air chamber or surge chamber, distributed the pressure to the pistons so they would pump evenly. Many people thought that these chrome or brass domes were there for decoration, but they were an important part of the steamers' equipment.

The horse-drawn steamer seemed to provide an efficient method of fighting fires, but it was soon to be replaced by something even more efficient. In the early 1900s, the gasoline-powered internal combustion engine appeared on the scene and began making changes in many areas of American life. The day of the horse was coming to an end, and before long, gasoline-driven tractors would be pulling steamers to fires.

Just as earlier firefighters had opposed the use of horses, so the firefighters of this period resisted the introduction of the bulky, ugly tractors. Races were held between horse-drawn steamers and steamers pulled by the gasoline-powered tractors. In the early days, when the gasoline engines had to be started by hand-cranking, the horses were often the first to arrive at a fire. But the invention of the electric starter eliminated this problem. The tractors, with their powerful engines,

A 1904 steamer with a brightly polished boiler

strong rubber tires, and easy maintenance, finally put the fire horses out of business.

Not long after the fire horse disappeared, the steam fire engine made its final run. Fire departments quickly discovered that gasoline engines could be used not only for driving vehicles but also for pumping water. In fact, a single engine could do both jobs, thus eliminating the need for a tractor and a separate piece of pumping equipment. Pumpers powered by gasoline motors were lighter, cleaner, and smaller than steamers. They were ready to go into action immediately, while steam engines needed time to build up pressure before they could begin pumping.

This steam fire engine is pulled by a gasoline-powered tractor.

By 1913, when this steam engine was built, steamers were being replaced by gasoline-driven pumpers.

By the end of the 1920s, horses and steamers were gone forever, and a colorful period of firefighting had become history. The steam whistles were silenced, and the gleaming boilers were left to tarnish until they were discovered by fire buffs who would polish and cherish them. Some buffs specialize in steam fire engines, but the number available to collectors is very small. Steamers are usually restored and operated by a group of collectors rather than by individuals. Shoveling coal and operating the controls of a steam fire engine are too much work for one person. Not many steamers can be seen in action at SPAAMFAA musters. Most of these beautiful machines are in museums, and their boilers haven't been fired up since the early 1900s.

PUMPERS

Gasoline-driven fire engines, usually called "pumpers," soon became the backbone of American fire departments. These engines were built with heavy-duty chassis, powerful motors, and pumps that took in water by suction and pumped it out under pressure. Pumpers had many advantages over the fire equipment of the past. They could be designed to suit the climates in which they would be used, they were smaller and more easily turned, and they could carry with them the hoses and other equipment necessary to fight most fires. Many different companies manufactured pumpers during the early 1900s, and some are still in business today. The small fire engines produced by these companies during the 1920s and 1930s are the ones that most fire buffs are interested in.

A few of these pumpers are pictured in the following pages.

The pumpers produced by the Ahrens-Fox Company were some of the most interesting of the 1920s and 1930s. Like the earlier steamers, these pumpers had surge chambers to regulate the action of the pistons and to get a steady flow of water from the hydrant. On the Ahrens-Fox pumper, the surge chamber was in the shape of a large chrome ball. The construction of this piece of equipment was a well-kept secret in the fire engine business. The ball was made in two separate pieces, and only one worker at the Ahrens-Fox plant knew how to join the halves together. At one time in the company's history, the man in charge of putting the ball together died suddenly without revealing his secret

This 1917 pumper manufactured by the White Company was famous for the shape of its radiator, which resembled an old-fashioned talcum-powder can.

method. Ahrens-Fox was in an uproar until the problem was solved.

The biggest rival of the Ahrens-Fox Company was the American LaFrance (ALF) Company, which built its first pumpers in 1910. Although Ahrens-Fox has stopped building fire trucks, American LaFrance continues to manufacture under the name of Ward LaFrance/Maxim. The company has produced many different kinds of fire engines since the early 1900s. One of the first ALF models built, the Type 10, was driven by a chain that ran from the motor to the wheels. The ALF Type 75 was a very popular pumper all over the United States.

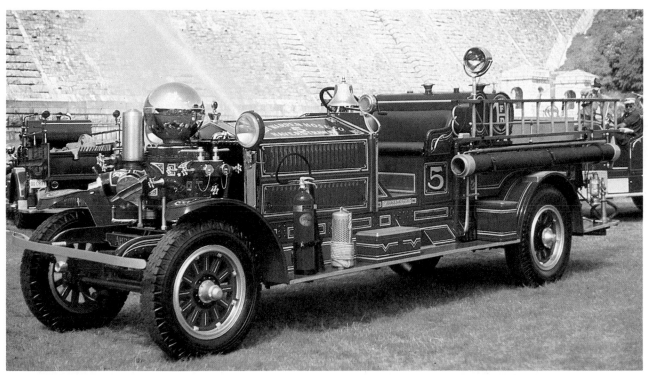

An Ahrens-Fox pumper from the 1920s. The round chrome surge chamber can be seen on the left side of the picture.

This 1923 Ahrens-Fox engine can pump 1,300 gallons of water per minute.

The Sugar Creek pumper

The 1927 ALF pumper shown here is a fire engine with a long and interesting history. Soon after it was built, the pumper was purchased by the town of Sugar Creek, Missouri. Sugar Creek was (and still is) the home of a big Standard Oil refinery, and the people of the community wanted to have a large, reliable fire engine available in case of a dangerous refinery fire. The 750-GPM ALF pumper suited their needs perfectly.

After many years of hard work, the Sugar Creek pumper was retired in the 1950s and sold to a small rural fire department. Several years later, it was sold again to a truck dealer, who repainted it and replaced the single wheels in the rear with dual wheels. At this point, the ALF pumper fell into the hands of a fire buff. I bought it in 1969 and took it to my hometown, Sugar Creek, Missouri, never guessing that I was returning the old pumper to its former home. It was not until I wrote Ward LaFrance/Maxim and gave them the engine's serial number that I realized the truth. After 20 years of absence, the old Sugar Creek pumper was home again, parked just five blocks from the fire house. And it was still capable of pumping a heavy stream of water.

Another pumper with a story to tell is this 1931 Reo-Nott quad. A quad is a fire engine that has four different functions: it pumps water, and it carries a chemical tank, hoses, and ladders. This 1931 model was originally purchased by a farmers' cooperative in a small Iowa community. Because it was to be used in a rural area, the quad was specially designed for heavy pulling in mud. Its top speed was only 40 miles an hour, but it could move through a field of thick goo as well as a tractor could. The truck carried a 400-gallon water tank and a 30-gallon chemical tank, plus many small pieces of firefighting equipment.

After 37 years of service, the Reo-Nott quad was sold in 1968 to a fire buff, who had seen it advertised in a paper selling antiques. The buff purchased the truck by mail and made a 400-mile drive to pick up his prize. He brought a heavy-duty trailer to carry the fire engine and a friend to help load it. The two men got the quad onto the trailer, but it was so heavy that it raised the car right off the ground. Finally, the buff decided he would have to drive the fire engine home, while his friend drove the car pulling the empty trailer.

The trip was quite an adventure. The headlights of the Reo-Nott failed, and the engine kept missing. It also made an awful racket because it didn't have a muffler. After 14 hours of driving through snow and freezing weather, the buff finally got his old pumper home.

The 1931 Reo-Nott quad after restoration. The buff has added a convertible top to his old fire engine.

When the restoration was started the next day, the collector discovered that the pumper's water tank was full of ice, which explained its excess weight. The problems with the engine were easily fixed, and a muffler was installed to keep peace with the local police. After three months of hard work, the fire buff was the proud owner of a pumper painted a bright rally red and decorated with 257 feet of gold striping. His old fire truck was fun and safe to drive (at speeds under 40 miles an hour), and it could still throw a steam of water at 500 GPM.

A close-up of the 1923 Ahrens-Fox pumper shown on page 30

Pumpers like this 1924 Graham were the pride of the small towns they served. Firefighters took very good care of them, right down to the varnished wood on their wheels.

AERIALS

Ladders have been part of American firefighting equipment since the colonial times, but they did not become really important until the 1800s. When buildings of several stories became common in American cities, ladders were needed to rescue people trapped on upper floors. The professional fire companies of the 1850s used long wooden ladders, which were carried on horse-drawn ladder trucks. The tall ladders were extremely heavy and difficult to lift into position. They were also dangerous to use because their bottom ends had a tendency to slip, toppling firefighters from their perches.

It was not until the end of the 1860s that the first "aerial" ladders were developed. Permanently mounted on a fire truck and raised by mechanical means, an aerial ladder was a safe and efficient piece of firefighting equipment. The first successful ladder of this kind was invented by Daniel Hayes, a worker in the repair shop of the San Francisco Fire Department. Hayes attached one end of a wooden ladder to a turntable mounted on a horse-drawn wagon. The ladder was raised by a crank-and-screw device, and it was placed against the side of a building by rotating the turntable. It could be extended by means of ropes and pulleys to a length of 100 feet.

In the 1880s, the American LaFrance Company bought the patent for Hayes' invention and began manufacturing aerial ladder equipment. Since that time, aerial trucks—usually just called "aerials"—have been used by most city fire departments in the United States. They have often served not only as a means of rescuing people but also as a kind of water tower, with hoses attached to the top of the tall ladders directing water on fires from above. There have been many developments in the methods used to raise the ladders and rotate the turntables, but the aerials of today operate on the same basic principle as the one invented by Daniel Hayes in the 1860s.

The aerials built by companies like American LaFrance and Ahrens-Fox during the early 1900s were a combination of tractor and trailer, totaling more than 50 feet in length. The trailer holding the ladder was so long that it was necessary to have a second driver in the rear to guide the aerial around corners. Most modern aerials no longer use the tractor-trailer combination, but are made up of a single unit.

A 1927 Ahrens-Fox aerial at a muster

This 1925 American LaFrance aerial is 65 feet long and has a place for a second driver in the rear.

Because most old aerials are so large, not many fire buffs have room for one in their garages. Some dedicated collectors, however, do buy and restore aerials. In 1968 two friends of mine acquired a pair of 1927 Ahrens-Fox aerials from the Kansas City Fire Department. They were tractor-trailer units with 75-foot ladders made out of solid pieces of pine. In addition to the enormous aerial ladder, each truck carried smaller wooden ladders of all kinds. One of the trucks had been used in fighting many industrial and warehouse fires, and every ladder on it smelled of smoke and pine resin. The fierce heat of the fires had caused the resin to bubble up out of the wood.

After buying the A-F aerials and driving them around a large parking lot for a while, my friends decided to sell the trucks rather than doing the restoration themselves. One aerial ended up in the St. Louis Transportation Museum, and the other was purchased by a SPAAMFAA member who lived in New York. This buff drove his 55-foot-long aerial home from Kansas City, with one of his sons steering the trailer from the rear driver's seat. The truck had a 10-gallon gas tank and got only 3 miles to the gallon, so every 30 miles, stops had to be made for refueling. At a top speed of 30 miles an hour, the 1,000-mile trip took four days.

The restoration took four months, and the

The restored 1927 Ahrens-Fox aerial that was driven from Kansas City to New York

A-F aerial was a smashing success at its first SPAAMFAA muster. The big aerial ladder pointed proudly at the sky just as it had during its 40 long years of firefighting service. From its top, a photographer took dramatic pictures of the muster, steadying himself while the heavy wooden ladder swayed in the slightest breeze. The buff who had restored the old aerial felt that his long drive and all his hard work had been worthwhile.

SERVICE TRUCKS

Service trucks did not get the glamorous firefighting jobs. They were usually in the background, out of the way of the aerials and pumpers, but they were important to the fire departments too. These trucks usually served a specific purpose. Some service trucks carried hoses, while others carried ladders and life nets or fire extinguishers. In most modern fire departments, a single truck handles all this equipment.

Sometimes, a special service truck would be custom-built if a community had a very particular need. In 1927 Ahrens-Fox designed a one-of-a-kind hose truck for use in the big Kansas City, Missouri, stockyards. Fire was a serious problem in the stockyards because of all the hay and other flammable materials around. The special A-F hose truck was much narrower and shorter than a normal fire truck, which allowed it to get into the animal pens and turn around in the small, cramped area. This unique service truck spent its entire working life in the Kansas City stockyards.

Other service trucks were not so unusual. One of the most common types was the Model 10 hose truck built by American LaFrance in the early 1900s. For many years, the fire department in Springfield, Missouri, had two 1913 ALF Model 10 trucks equipped with gas lamps and chain drive. The community used the hose trucks for such a long time that they were eventually refitted with electric lights and electric starters.

In the 1930s, these two service trucks were purchased by an antique car collector, who converted one of the trucks into a

The A-F hose truck used in the Kansas City stockyards

"speedster," an early form of hot rod. Many Model 10 ALFs suffered this fate. The fire equipment was removed, the big wheels were cut down, and two open seats were installed. Today both the Springfield Model 10 hose trucks are in the hands of fire buffs who are restoring them to their original condition.

Carrying chemical fire extinguishers was another job sometimes performed by service trucks. These devices were first developed in the 1870s and were used in cities to fight small fires or in rural areas where water was in short supply. Today extinguishers are also used in fighting electric fires or those involving flammable liquids such as oil or gasoline.

Most of the chemical extinguishers used in the past were of the soda-acid type. They combined bicarbonate of soda, sulfuric acid, and water to create the gas carbon dioxide. Sprayed out through small hoses under pressure, the carbon dioxide smothered a fire by removing the oxygen necessary for combustion. There were several ways of combining these three ingredients and producing carbon dioxide. The most common system used a large metal tank containing solution of soda and water. Within the tank was suspended a small bottle of sulfuric acid, which was added to the soda-water solution at the time the extinguisher was to be used. The acid was released from its container by pulling a lever or by turning the whole tank upside down and dumping the acid into the solution.

The heavy metal tanks that contained the chemicals were often mounted on trucks in a horizontal position. Each tank had a chrome wheel at one end, much like the wooden steering wheel of an old ship. Firefighters used the wheel to turn the tank over and mix the chemicals. A service truck also carried smaller tanks, about the size of modern portable fire extinguishers, which contained extra soda. These small chrome or nickel tanks were mounted on the truck's rear running board.

The chrome wheel on the chemical tank of this service truck can be seen on the right side of the photograph.

This 1930 Fargo Express service truck carried hoses, ladders, and chemical tanks.

The trucks that carried chemical fire extinguishers were often very small. In the early 1900s, little Model T Ford trucks were used by many fire departments. Later, some departments carried chemical tanks along with other equipment, as on the Fargo Express shown here. This 1930 Chrysler-built truck had a hose compartment in the back and two large chemical tanks behind the driver's seat. Ladders were mounted on the side. This particular Fargo Express has been restored to a thing of beauty by a dedicated fire buff. Restoring a chemical extinguisher truck usually requires a lot of repainting due to damage caused by the harsh chemical solutions.

These photographs show a variety of fire trucks manufactured since the 1920s. *Top left:* 1923 Sanford; *top right:* 1924 Mack; *bottom left:* 1941 GMC; *bottom right:* 1965 Walters.

CONCLUSION

Firefighting equipment has been greatly improved since the days of the first hand-pumped fire engines. Powerful new kinds of pumps and aerials operated by hydraulic power have made the firefighter's job easier. Many American fire departments now use such sophisticated firefighting tools as foam, dry chemical extinguishers, and hose nozzles that turn a stream of water into a "fog" made up of tiny droplets. Modern firefighters also use "wet water" to extinguish certain kinds of fire. Made by mixing chemicals with ordinary water, wet water soaks into such materials as hay or baled cotton instead of beading up and rolling off as plain water does.

Today's firefighting equipment has become so complicated and expensive that it will probably not end up in the hands of collectors. Instead, the members of SPAAMFAA will continue to collect and restore yesterday's fire engines — the steamers, pumpers, and aerials from a simpler period of American life.

Superwheels & Thrill Sports

Lerner Publications Company
241 First Avenue North, Minneapolis, Minnesota 55401